The Elves' Night Before Christmas

By Holly Kowitt
and David Manis

Illustrated by
Richard Watson

SCHOLASTIC INC.

'Twas the night before Christmas,
and all Santa's elves
were tired, but feeling
quite proud of themselves.

Then one cried, "Wait a minute!
There's someone we missed . . .
the most favorite person
on everyone's list!"

What would Santa want?
He wasn't a kid.

So they went to their workshop,
and here's what they did:

Sue made him a sandwich
eleven feet tall.
(The bread couldn't really
keep hold of it all.)

Tom washed his red suit.
It came out squeaky clean,
but somehow it shrunk
in the washing machine.

Dwayne's reindeer whistle
would signal the team . . .

Although, to the reindeer,
it's quite loud, it seems.

Philip's statue of snow
would be known nationwide . . .

If only he hadn't
brought it inside.

Kate made a big star
for the top of the tree . . .
A little bit *too* big,
if you ask me.

A ski jump to start
Santa's flight with a leap!
Raúl tested it out . . .

It might be too steep.

Liz made fancy labels!
She mixed them up, though . . .
so a present for Janie
might end up with Joe.

A gift-wrap machine
that everything fits in . . .
But then Clara couldn't find
Rudolph or Blitzen!

Lee jazzed up the sleigh,
now it only flies zigzag . . .

Which made all the presents
fall out of the big bag!

Then a knock at the door —
and Santa walked in.
How to explain this?
Where to begin?

"We made you these gifts.
A few were mistakes.
We lost a few reindeer.
We had some bad breaks."

"How about something else?
We have box after box!
Fingernail clippers!
Cuckoo-bird clocks!"

"Snowshoes! Hula-Hoops!
Exercise kits!
CDs of the best
karaoke elf hits!"

"We're sorry!" they wailed.
"Please, please understand
the gifts we made
didn't work out like we planned!"

But Santa spoke up:
"No more crying! Please stop!
I love what you did
'cause it came from the heart."

So they ironed his suit,
then fixed up his sleigh,
and made him hot chocolate
to drink on his way.

Then Santa called out
as he flew out of sight,
"Merry Christmas to all,
and to all a good night!"